Big Book of Christmas Stories

Miles Kelly

First published in 2015 by Miles Kelly Publishing Ltd
Harding's Barn, Bardfield End Green, Thaxted, Essex, CM6 3PX, UK

This edition printed 2016

4 6 8 10 9 7 5 3

Publishing Director Belinda Gallagher
Creative Director Jo Cowan
Editorial Director Rosie Neave
Editors Fran Bromage, Amy Johnson
Design Manager Joe Jones
Production Elizabeth Collins, Caroline Kelly
Reprographics Stephan Davis, Jennifer Cozens, Thom Allaway
Assets Lorraine King

ISBN 978-1-78617-161-0

Printed in China

British Library Cataloguing-in-Publication Data
A catalogue record for this book is available from the British Library

ACKNOWLEDGEMENTS
The publishers would like to thank the following artists who have contributed to this book:
Advocate Art: Luciana Feito (The Nutcracker) and Claire Keay (The Snow Queen)
Lemonade Illustration Agency: Luis Filella (The Twelve Days of Christmas)
The Organisation: Yorgos Sgouros (The First Christmas)
Endpapers: smilewithjul/Shutterstock.com

Made with paper from a sustainable forest

www.mileskelly.net

The First Christmas

A long time ago, a young woman called Mary lived in the little town of Nazareth. She was engaged to marry a carpenter named Joseph.

One day, Mary was visited by an angel, who told her that she would have a very special baby. The baby would be the son of God, and he was to be called Jesus.

The angel also visited Joseph in a dream.

"Mary's child will be the saviour of God's people," the angel told him.

"You should raise him as your own."

Just before the birth, Mary and Joseph had to travel to Bethlehem, Joseph's birthplace, to be counted in a survey.

It was a very long way to
Bethlehem, and when they arrived it
was late. The streets were crowded with
people who had also come to be counted.

Mary and Joseph began to look
for an inn to stay in,

as the baby was about
to be born.

They tried many places, but everywhere was full.

Growing desperate, Mary and Joseph tried the very last inn.

"I'm sorry," the innkeeper said,
"but there are no rooms left.

All I can offer you is my stable."

Mary and Joseph
were very grateful.

That night, in the warm stable amongst the animals, Mary gave birth to a baby boy.

She called him Jesus, just as the angel had said. Carefully, she wrapped him in cloths and laid him in the

manger.

Meanwhile, on the hills just outside Bethlehem, some shepherds were watching over their flock.

Suddenly, an angel appeared.
"I bring wonderful news.
A child has been born who will
be the saviour of all people."

As the shepherds watched, amazed, the sky was filled with hundreds of

dazzling angels

all singing songs of joy.

The angel told the shepherds that
they would find the baby in a stable in
Bethlehem. They hurried straight
there, very excited.

When they reached the stable, there was
Jesus in the manger. The shepherds
believed that he truly was the saviour.

Some time after Jesus was born, in distant lands, three wise men saw a new star in the night sky. It shone much more brightly than the rest.

They knew what this meant – a child had been born who would be the king of God's people.

They set off at once to find him, following the new star.

In Jerusalem, the wise men were summoned to see King Herod. He had heard about the new king, and was not happy.

He ordered them to tell him where the baby was once they had found him.

When the wise men reached Bethlehem, the star shone above a small house. Inside, the wise men bowed before Jesus and gave him gifts of gold, frankincense and myrrh.

On their journey home, the wise men did not return to King Herod, as they had a dream that warned them not to.

An angel then appeared to Joseph to warn him of danger, so the family set off for Egypt. There Jesus, the saviour, would be safe.

24

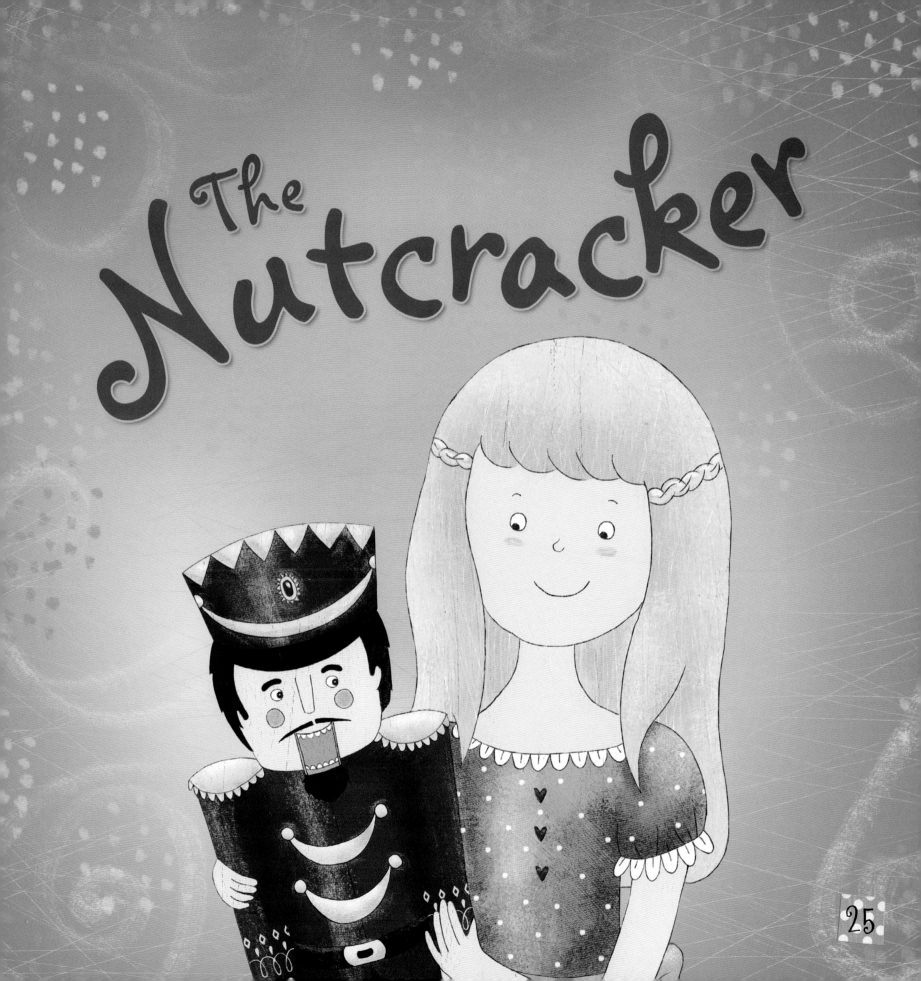

The Nutcracker

It was Christmas Eve, and Clara was
staring out of the window at the snow
falling on to the icy ground outside.

Inside, the Christmas party
was starting. Everything looked
twinkly and magical. Clara's
brother, Franz, and her cousins
ran around excitedly.

Suddenly Clara's godfather appeared. He was a toymaker and he always made the children beautiful toys. "Merry Christmas!" he cried and handed presents to all the children.

To Clara he gave the best present of all. "He's a very special nutcracker," whispered Clara's godfather.

The Nutcracker looked like a toy soldier, but he could crack nuts with his teeth. Franz tried to crack a huge walnut, but suddenly the Nutcracker's jaw snapped!

CRACK!

Clara began to cry. "Don't worry," said her
godfather, tying his handkerchief around
the Nutcracker's jaw. "I'll mend
him properly in the morning."

Soon it was time for bed. Clara laid her
Nutcracker under the tree with the
other toys, but she couldn't sleep
thinking about her broken toy.

Clara crept downstairs, and snuggled down next to the tree with her Nutcracker. She quickly fell asleep.

Suddenly, there was a loud creaking sound! Clara woke to find the Nutcracker and the toy soldiers had grown.

"Hello, I'm the Nutcracker Prince," he said, bowing to Clara.

34

"I'm here to protect you,"
said the Nutcracker Prince.
Clara heard a scuttling sound
and a mouse army crept
out of the shadows.

Immediately, the toy soldiers and
the Nutcracker Prince drew
their swords. With a loud squeak, the
36 Mouse King charged and the battle began.

"I have to help," said Clara. Amid the shouts and clanging of swords, Clara took off a slipper and threw it at the Mouse King.

The Mouse King fell to the ground. There was a moment of silence, then the other mice scuttled away.

Clara stared in amazement as the Nutcracker became a handsome Prince.

"Your bravery broke the Mouse King's spell," said the Prince. "I've been trapped as a toy for years, but now I'm free!" The Prince handed Clara the Mouse King's crown.

"We must celebrate!" said the Prince as he called for his magical sleigh and reindeer. Clara's nightgown turned into a beautiful ballgown.

The Prince and Clara flew through the air
in the sleigh. They sailed through the snowy night
until they reached the Land of Sweets.

Soon the sleigh came to a stop in front
of a castle. A Sugar Plum Fairy
was waiting for them.
"Welcome to the Marzipan Palace!" she said.

The Prince told the
Sugar Plum Fairy
how Clara had saved him.
"We must have a banquet
in your honour," she cried,
clapping her hands.

The banquet was astounding. There were cakes, cookies, sweets and fancies from every corner of the world.

As they feasted, dancers from every country whirled, pranced and jumped. Clara stared in amazement.

All too soon it was time for the final dance. The Prince and the Sugar Plum Fairy walked to the centre of the floor and performed a

magnificent waltz.

Clara thought they looked beautiful. She curled up in her chair to watch the dancers and the flecks of light moving with them. Slowly, Clara's eyes began to close.

When Clara woke up she was at home again, under the Christmas tree. The Prince was gone, but her nutcracker toy was lying in her arms, his jaw fixed into a knowing smile.

The Snow Queen

There were once two best friends, Gerda and Kay. They told each other everything, and everywhere they went, they went together.

"Hello Kay!"

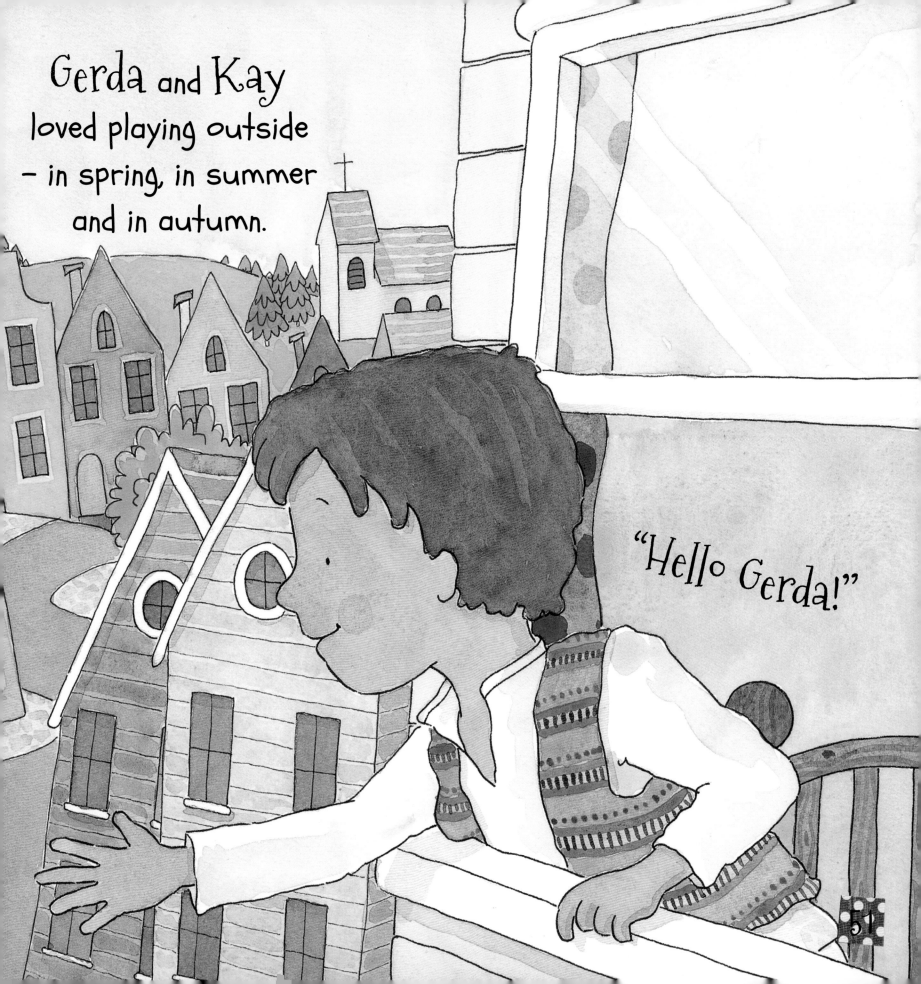

Gerda and Kay loved playing outside – in spring, in summer and in autumn.

"Hello Gerda!"

51

But Winter was their favourite season. Grandmother told the best stories during the cold evenings. One night, the story was about the

Snow Queen.

52

"The Snow Queen lives in a huge snow palace,"
said Grandmother. "Her enchanted snow settles deep
in your heart, so you forget who you are."

That night, Kay couldn't sleep. He kept thinking about the Snow Queen. He opened his window to peer down at the icy street.

In that moment, the Snow Queen threw down a speck of enchanted snow and captured Kay's heart.

55

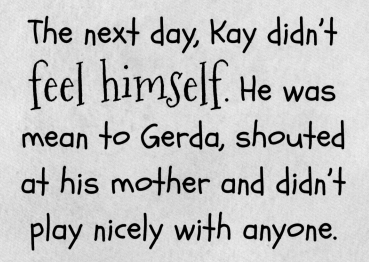

The next day, Kay didn't **feel himself.** He was mean to Gerda, shouted at his mother and didn't play nicely with anyone.

As each day passed, Kay seemed to find new ways to be horrible. The Snow Queen's enchantment was working its magic.

Then, one morning as Kay played alone, a huge, sparkling sleigh appeared over the hill.

The Snow Queen had come to snatch Kay away.

When Gerda came to look for him, Kay was gone. Gerda searched everywhere but Kay wasn't in the village any more.

Gerda was certain the Snow Queen had stolen Kay away. So, she left the village to search for him.

Kaaa   kaaa!

After many miles,
Gerda met a raven.
"I've seen your friend,"
said the raven.

"He's with the Snow
Queen at her palace."

61

Gerda followed the raven deep into a forest. Suddenly rOBBerS appeared. Thinking her rich, they stole Gerda's things, and bundled her into a cart.

They took Gerda to their house and locked her in a barn.

A little robber girl lived there too, and she showed Gerda all the animals she looked after.

63

Gerda told the robber girl about her search for Kay. That night, the girl helped Gerda escape so she could continue her journey.

The robber girl gave Gerda her favourite reindeer to ride, and a warm cloak to wear.

"My reindeer will show you the way to the Snow Palace," said the girl.

67

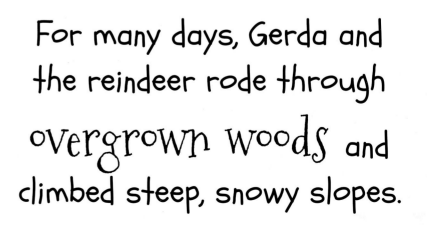

For many days, Gerda and the reindeer rode through **overgrown woods** and climbed steep, snowy slopes.

At last, frozen and exhausted, Gerda arrived at the magnificent Snow Palace.

67

Gerda felt very scared, but she loved and missed Kay very much. She pushed open the doors to the Snow Palace and went inside.

Sitting on the frozen floor in the middle of an icy room was Kay. He was staring into space, and didn't recognize Gerda at all!

69

"Oh Kay," cried Gerda dropping to her knees, "how can I help you?" But Kay didn't move. Exhausted, Gerda curled up by her friend and cried herself to sleep.

As Gerda slept, her tears warmed Kay's hands. The ice began to melt and Gerda's love for Kay thawed the enchanted snow!

Suddenly, Gerda felt Kay hug her tightly.

"I remember you," he said, and the best friends ran laughing from the melting Snow Palace.

The Twelve Days of Christmas

On the first day
of Christmas my
true love gave to me,

a partridge in
a pear tree.

On the second day of Christmas my true love gave to me,

two turtle doves

and a partridge in a pear tree.

On the third day of Christmas
my true love gave to me,

three French hens,

two turtle doves and a partridge in a pear tree.

On the fourth day of Christmas
my true love gave to me,

four calling birds,

three French hens,
two turtle doves
and a partridge in
a pear tree.

On the fifth day of Christmas
my true love gave to me,

five gold rings,

four calling birds, three French hens,
two turtle doves and
a partridge in a pear tree.

On the sixth day of Christmas
my true love gave to me,

six geese a-laying,

five gold rings, four calling birds,
three French hens, two turtle doves
and a partridge in a pear tree.

On the seventh day of Christmas
my true love gave to me,

seven swans
a-swimming,

Six geese a-laying, five gold rings,
four calling birds, three French hens,
two turtle doves and
a partridge in a pear tree.

Seven swans a-swimming,
six geese a-laying,
five gold rings, four calling birds,
three French hens, two turtle doves
and a partridge in a pear tree.

On the ninth day of Christmas
my true love gave to me,

nine ladies dancing,
eight maids a-milking,
seven swans a-swimming,

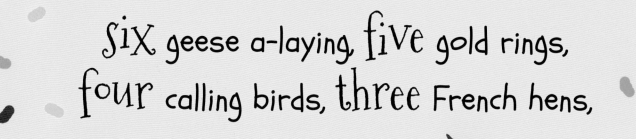

Six geese a-laying, five gold rings,
four calling birds, three French hens,

two turtle doves
and a partridge in a pear tree.

On the tenth day of Christmas
my true love gave to me,

ten lords
    a-leaping,

nine ladies dancing,
eight maids a-milking,

Seven swans a-swimming,
six geese a-laying,
five gold rings, four calling birds,
three French hens, two turtle doves
and a partridge in a pear tree.

On the eleventh day of Christmas
my true love gave to me,

eleven pipers piping,

ten lords a-leaping
nine ladies dancing

92

eight maids a-milking, seven swans a-swimming,
six geese a-laying, five gold rings,
four calling birds, three French hens,
two turtle doves and a partridge in a pear tree.

93

On the twelfth day of Christmas
my true love gave to me,

twelve drummers drumming,

eleven pipers piping,
ten lords a-leaping,
nine ladies dancing,
eight maids a-milking,
seven swans a-swimming,

94

Six geese a-laying, five gold rings, four calling birds,
three French hens, two turtle doves
and a partridge in a pear tree.